The text in this edition of *Panda Bear, Panda Bear, What Do You See?* has been reformatted for beginning readers.

A Note on Endangered Species

We are losing our animals. More than 5,000 animal species are endangered or threatened worldwide. This means that they are in danger of disappearing forever.

To safeguard these animals, there are over 3,500 protected areas in the form of parks, wildlife refuges, and other reserves around the world. This book features ten of these endangered or threatened species.

We can all help save them by spreading the word about conservation.

The author wishes to thank Michael Sampson for his help in the preparation of this text.

The Eric Carle Museum of Picture Book Art was built to celebrate the art that we are first exposed to as children. Located in Amherst, Massachusetts, the 40,000-square-foot museum is the first in the United States devoted to national and international picture book art.

Visit www.carlemuseum.org

Visit mackids.com/series/MyFirstReader/BillMartinJr to learn about Bill Martin Jr's approach to reading.

Henry Holt and Company, LLC
Publishers since 1866
175 Fifth Avenue
New York, New York 10010
www.HenryHoltKids.com

Library of Congress Cataloging-in-Publication Data
Martin, Bill, 1916–2004.
Panda bear, panda bear, what do you see? / by Bill Martin Jr. ; pictures by Eric Carle.
p.   cm. — (My first reader)
Summary: Illustrations and rhyming text present ten different endangered animals in this easy-reader version of the 2003 tale. Includes note to parents and teachers, as well as activities.
ISBN 978-0-8050-9292-9 (paper over board : alk. paper)
[1. Stories in rhyme. 2. Endangered species—Fiction. 3. Animals—Fiction.] I. Carle, Eric, ill. II. Title.
PZ8.3.M3988Pan 2011   [E]—dc22   2010011694

First hardcover edition—2003
First My First Reader edition—2011
Printed in October 2010 in China by South China Printing Company Ltd.,
Dongguan City, Guangdong Province, on acid-free paper. ∞

10 9 8 7 6 5 4 3 2 1

PANDA BEAR, PANDA BEAR, WHAT DO YOU SEE?

By Bill Martin Jr
Pictures by Eric Carle

Henry Holt and Company · New York

Panda Bear,
Panda Bear,
what do you see?

I see a bald eagle
soaring by me.

Bald Eagle,
Bald Eagle,
what do you see?

I see a water buffalo
charging by me.

Water Buffalo,
Water Buffalo,
what do you see?

I see a spider monkey
swinging by me.

8

Spider Monkey,
Spider Monkey,
what do you see?

I see a green sea turtle
swimming by me.

Green Sea Turtle,
Green Sea Turtle,
what do you see?

I see a macaroni penguin
strutting by me.

12

Macaroni Penguin,
Macaroni Penguin,
what do you see?

I see a sea lion
splashing by me.

Sea Lion,
Sea Lion,
what do you see?

I see a red wolf
sneaking by me.

Red Wolf,
Red Wolf,
what do you see?

I see a whooping crane
flying by me.

Whooping Crane,
Whooping Crane,
what do you see?

I see a black panther
strolling by me.

Black Panther,
Black Panther,
what do you see?

I see a dreaming child
watching over me.

Dreaming Child,
Dreaming Child,
what do you see?

I see…

a panda bear,   a bald eagle,

a green sea turtle,   a macaroni penguin,

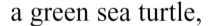

a whooping crane,   and a black panther…

24

a water buffalo, a spider monkey,

a sea lion, a red wolf,

**all wild and free—
that's what I see.**

25

Dear Parents and Teachers,

Panda Bear, Panda Bear, What Do You See? is a
patterned, question-and-answer book. These qualities can
be helpful to children learning to read because the repetitive
language along with word clues in Eric Carle's pictures help
children to predict what happens next, to remember the story,
and to learn to read many of the words easily.

Here are some ways that you might use this book with
children:

+ Before opening the book, talk about the panda bear
  on the cover. Ask, "What might Panda Bear see?"
+ Next, turn the pages and enjoy the bold collage
  art together. Ask, "What do you know about
  this animal?"
+ After you read and reread the story many times,
  pause before an animal or an action word and
  encourage your child to supply that word. If your
  child doesn't chime in, try again on another day.
+ See the following pages for more activities.

When your child says, "I want to read this book by
myself!" celebrate the reading and listen with enthusiasm
as your child reads it again and again.

—Laura Robb
Educator and Reading Consultant

27

What animal names
can you read?

panda bear

bald eagle

water buffalo

spider monkey

green sea turtle

Can you match the words
to the pictures?

macaroni penguin

sea lion

red wolf

whooping crane

black panther

What action words can you read?

soar

charge

swing

swim

strut

Can you act
them out?

splash

sneak

fly

stroll

watch

31

Which animals like
to be in cold places?

Which animals like
to be in warm places?

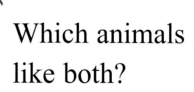

Which animals
like both?

Which animals like
to be in water?

Which animals like
to stay on land?

Which animals
like both?

E   Martin, Bill, 1916–
    2004.

    Panda bear, panda
    bear, what do you
    see?

DATE

BAKER & TAYLOR